MW00897894

Monster Lesson to Stay Cool
Written by Steve Herman.

ISBN: 978-1-948040-54-9 (paperback)
ISBN: 978-1-948040-55-6 (hardcover)
ISBN: 978-1-948040-56-3 (ebook)

First Edition: October 2018
10 9 8 7 6 5 4 3 2 1

www.MonsterLesson.com

I'm Max, and there's something unique about me - or about my best friend: he's a monster, you see.

Moe lives in a picture that hangs on my wall. Though he looks really scary, he's not bad at all.

He comes out of his picture and sits in my chair.
He's oodles of fun, he's frank, and he's fair.

And I had to wait in the hot, hot sun, at the end of the line, behind everyone.

Another day I went with Mom to the store.
I asked for some games, but my mom said, "No more."

That made me so mad. "But I want them!" I said.
My fists tightly clenched and my face turned red.

"Give them back!" I demanded, "Those aren't yours; they're mine!"
As I snatched them away, Markie started to whine,

And soon he was crying; I knew I was doomed.
"OK, Max," said Mom, "You can go to your room."

I stomped up to my room and slammed shut my door.
Moe jumped down beside me: "Wow, Max, you're sure sore!

"What's bothering you?" he asked thoughtfully.
And I told him the bad things that happened to me.

Moe listened to all that I had to say,
And then took my hand in a friendly way.

I was sure that Moe would be on my side,
So I was surprised when he replied...

"And how many games does one boy need?
You have plenty of toys, Max - many indeed!
You don't really need a new game to play.
You have more than you need; you could give some away!"

"And you're bigger than Markie; he looks up to you! So, be someone he can look up to!"

When Moe finished talking, and all was quiet,
I thought for a moment, and I told Moe, "You're right."

I went down right away, handed Markie my toy.
He smiled up at me and then jumped for joy.

This morning at breakfast I promised my mom, "I'll try very hard to stay calm from now on."

At school, Ms. Rogers smiled happily,
When I let Katie slide down ahead of me.

To lose patience and to become angry, you see, is not good for others, and it's not good for me!

35089628R00022

Made in the USA
Middletown, DE
01 February 2019